CHOSEN BY
GABY MORGAN

Fairy
Poems

MACMILLAN CHILDREN'S BOOKS

For Lizzie Broadbent

First published 2006 by Macmillan Children's Books

This edition published 2010 by Macmillan Children's Books
a division of Macmillan Publishers Limited
20 New Wharf Road, London N1 9RR
Basingstoke and Oxford
Associated companies throughout the world
www.panmacmillan.com

ISBN 978-0-330-51876-5

1 3 5 7 9 8 6 4 2

A CIP catalogue record for this book is available from
the British Library.

Printed and bound in the UK by CPI Mackays, Chatham ME5 8TD

Contents

Fairy Names

What shall we call the Fairy Child?

Mouse-Fur? Cat's Purr?
Weasel-Wild?

Bat-Wing? Bee-Sting?
Shining River?
Snakebite? Starlight?
Stone? Or Shiver?

Acorn? Frogspawn?
Golden Tree?
Snowflake? Daybreak?
Stormy Sea?

Snail-Shell? Harebell?
Scarlet Flame?

How shall we choose the Fairy's name?

Clare Bevan

The Fairy Queen

The fairy queen sits on her throne,
paler than the mist,
a flower wreath about her head,
a berry bracelet, ruby red,
twined about her wrist.

Her wings are gauzy, rainbow laced,
her hair as dark as night.
Her dress of cobwebs, softly grey,
dewdrop sprinkled, bright as day,
gives forth an eldritch light.

Her wand glows with a single star,
her eyes are fathomless pools.
Her breath is flower, fern and spice,
but her heart is flint and ice
and her smile is cruel.

She will lead the wild, wild dance
through the fairy glades,
as she has done time out of mind,
beyond the ken of humankind,
since the world was made.

Marian Swinger

Wish

She wished she could fly.
She wished for friends
who were birds and flowers.
She wished she wore a silver frock.

She wished she could speak
with a magic tongue.
She wished so hard.
She wished so hard.

Now she works
in the baker's shop.
She wears a white coat
and a netted cap.

She speaks the language
of mam and dad
and at the end of each day
her feet hurt.

But at night she carries her baby
up to the stars. She sings to him
in the language of flowers.
He reaches out to touch her silver wings.

Mandy Coe

A Fairy Carol for Summer

the love fairy and I
will sing all this summer

sun is her ringfort
brave and unbroken

field is her green table
clouds are her white saucers

winds are her pale ribbons
trailing seed aircraft

no rain from the west
will douse her fire-flowers

her days are alive
and her nights are so sleepless

the love fairy and I
will dance all this summer

John Rice

Will o' the Wisp

It haunts the marshes and the bogs
And in the creeping mists and fogs
Takes eerie, mischievous delight
In offering its wandering light
To travellers who have lost their way –
Leading them only worse astray.

Eric Finney

Flower Fairies

These gentle spirits of the earth
Live for kindness, beauty, mirth.
Such gifts they'll spread with faery powers
To all who take delight in flowers.

Eric Finney

Pilliwiggin

Where to look for Pilliwiggin?
I'd advise you to begin
By spending time (it may take hours)
Just peeping in the bells of flowers
For Pilliwiggins take a kip
In wild thyme, bluebell and cowslip.

Eric Finney

Dryad

Pale primroses I planted
By the great oak tree
And when they bloomed in Springtime
The Dryad sang to me.
Sang a curious music
To the ears of belief,
Music of bole and branch and twig,
Of bursting bud and leaf.

Eric Finney

Bean Tighe

(pronounced 'Ban Teeg')

Aren't I just the lucky one!
Bean Tighe has settled in my home.
Expert faery housekeeper,
Cook, cleaner, carpet sweeper.
Seeks a friendly household – yours?
Then will handle all chores.
Just attract a Bean Tighe –
Forget all worry, stress, fatigue.

Eric Finney

Churnmilk Peg

This fairy, Yorkshire folk allege,
Guards hazelnuts upon the hedge.
Pick them unripe and she will make
The pickers suffer bellyache.

Eric Finney

Alp Luachra

Don't fall asleep by the side of a stream
Or this bad Irish fairy, shaped like a newt,
Will crawl in your mouth while you slumber and
dream
And feed off your food – meat, veg and fruit.
The outcome of that I'll leave you to guess –
But your weight could crash-dive to considerably
less.

Eric Finney

Leprechaun

See him in leather apron
Working at his trade:
By this fairy cobbler
The shoes of elves are made.
He wears a natty suit of green
Topped with a smart red hat –
All in all a splendid fellow:
You might well think that.
But come the night this little sprite,
When his long day's work is done,
Becomes, I am afraid to say,
a bit of a hooligan.
He's into feasting, drinking,
Down in the wine cellar:
Such riotous behaviour
Paints quite a different fellow.
And late at night he may be seen
Riding the moonlit skies
Mounted upon a sheep or dog
Towards the new sunrise.

Eric Finney

Somewhere in the World

Between the blue of a sparkling sea
And the azure of a summer sky,
The snow-white wings of fairy-terns
Filter sunlight as they fly.

Between the seaweed in sandy rock pools,
If you had the eyes of a hungry fish,
You might see the dainty fairy-shrimp
Dart out of reach to a rocky niche.

Between the blades of daisied grass
Where there's a stranger, darker green
Is the emerald mark of a fairy-ring,
Though no fairies can be seen.

Between the silver of the moon
And the street lamps' pools of golden light
When ghost-moths flitter, you might believe
You've seen fairies dance, and you may be right.

And – if you knew just where to look
And you made a promise not to tell
You might discover and make a wish
In the secret water of a fairy-well.

Catherine Benson

The Water Sprites

Who are these three
I can almost see
Down by the river
Where the tall reeds quiver?

They speak in voices
Like watery noises,
Lip-lapping,
Slip-slapping.

Who are these three?

One seems tall
And one seems small,
The other has
No shape at all.

Who are these three?

Do they live by the waters,
These three strange daughters?
Are they made from air?
I know they are there.

Who are these three
I can almost see
Down by the river,
Where the tall reeds quiver?

Gerard Benson

A Lake and a Fairy Boat

A lake and a fairy boat
To sail in the moonlight clear,
And merrily we would float
From the dragons that watch us here!

Thy gown should be snow-white silk;
And strings of orient pearls,
Like gossamers dipped in milk,
Should twine with thy raven curls!

Red rubies should deck thy hands,
And diamonds should be thy dower –
But Fairies have broke their wands,
And wishing has lost its power!

Thomas Hood

Marsh Sprite

It's not about
the inky night and the miles
of bubbling marsh, it's this
heartbeat when you glimpse
a small blue light and decide
whether to lay down your foot
a little to the left or
a little to the right.

They say this hungry mud
will swallow a horse
before it takes fright, so
you'll trust the stars, the whisper
of reeds – anything, even
this little blue light.

Lift one foot and start
the long journey home.
Please little light be true.
Please be true little light.

Mandy Coe

Overheard on a Saltmarsh

Nymph, nymph, what are your beads?

Green glass, goblin. Why do you stare at them?

Give them me.

No.

Give them me. Give them me.

No.

Then I will howl all night in the reeds,
Lie in the mud and howl for them.

Goblin, why do you love them so?

They are better than stars or water,
Better than voices of winds that sing,
Better than any man's fair daughter,
Your green glass beads on a silver ring.

Hush, I stole them out of the moon.

Give me your beads, I want them.

No.

I will howl in a deep lagoon
For your green glass beads, I love them so.
Give them me. Give them.

                    No.

                    Harold Monro

Fairy Bread

Come up here, O dusty feet!
  Here is fairy bread to eat.
Here in my retiring room,
  Children you may dine
On the golden smell of broom
  And the shade of pine;
And when you have eaten well,
  Fairy stories hear and tell.

        Robert Louis Stevenson

The Sea-Fairies

Slow sail'd the weary mariners and saw,
Betwixt the green brink and the running foam,
Sweet faces, rounded arms, and bosoms prest
To little harps of gold; and while they mused,
Whispering to each other half in fear,
Shrill music reach'd on the middle sea.

Whither away, whither away, whither away? fly no
    more.
Whither away, from the high green field, and the
    happy blossoming shore?
Day and night to the billow the fountain calls;
Down shower the gambolling waterfalls
From wandering over the lea;
Out of the live-green heart of the dells
They freshen the silvery-crimson shells,
And thick with white bells the clover-hill swells
High over the full-toned sea.
O, hither, come hither and furl your sails,
Come hither to me and to me;
Hither, come hither and frolic and play;
Here it is only the mew that wails;
We will sing to you all the day.
Mariner, mariner, furl your sails,
For here are the blissful downs and dales,
And merrily, merrily carol the gales,
And the spangle dances in bight and bay,

And the rainbow forms and flies on the land
Over the islands free;
And the rainbow lives in the curve of the sand;
Hither, come hither and see;
And the rainbow hangs on the poisoning wave,
And sweet is the colour of cove and cave,
And sweet shall your welcome be.
O, hither, come hither, and be our lords,
For merry brides are we.
We will kiss sweet kisses, and speak sweet words;
O, listen, listen, your eyes shall glisten
With pleasure and love and jubilee.
O, listen, listen, your eyes shall glisten
When the sharp clear twang of the golden chords
Runs up the ridged sea.
Who can light on as happy a shore
All the world o'er, all the world o'er?
Whither away? listen and stay; mariner, mariner, fly
    no more.

Alfred, Lord Tennyson

Sea Fairies

In spray and foam and splashing tide
on white horse waves Sea Fairies ride
and follow ships across the deep
to find the place where children sleep.

Then when the sun has gone to rest,
they do the thing that they do best.
They snuggle warm inside your dreams
and visit places where it seems
in magic castles in the air
all dreams come true once you are there.

But all too soon the sun will rise
to waken little sleepy eyes
and with a kiss they'll slip away
to ride and race another day.

Brian D'Arcy

Sugar Plum Fairies Dance

In forest glade and orchard wood,
at break of day when birdsong rings,
all children can, if they are good,
see fairy folk on whisper wings
rise dreamily in perfumed hues
of golden days and midnight blues.

And peeping from each blossomed branch,
aglow with promises of fruits,
sugar plum fairies wait to dance
to music played on magic flutes.
Their dresses cast in perfumed hues
are colours only fairies choose.

So when you hear that woodland sound,
however close or far away,
move carefully for all around
small fairies dance to greet the day,
while scattering in perfumed hue
bright rainbow jewels in drops of dew.

Brian D'Arcy

The Fairy's Song

Over hill, over dale,
Thorough bush, thorough brier,
Over park, over pale,
Thorough flood, thorough fire,
I do wander everywhere,
Swifter than the moonés sphere;
And I serve the fairy queen,
To dew her orbs upon the green.
The cowslips tall her pensioners be;
In their gold coats spots you see;
Those be rubies, fairy favours,
In those freckles live their savours.
I must go seek some dewdrops here,
And hang a pearl in every cowslip's ear.

William Shakespeare

Midnight Fairy

I am the Midnight Fairy,
I float between the stars.
I dance among the planets
from Mercury to Mars.

My gown's a swirl of sparklers
you call the Milky Way.
It flutters through the sky from dusk
until the break of day.

My wings have silver feathers
to fly me to the moon.
Their flutter is the music
of my Midnight Fairy tune.

My eyes are deepest sapphire,
my long, long black hair streams;
and if you want to see me,
just look inside your dreams.

Alison Chisholm

Tam Lin

Don't go down to Carterhaugh,
Carterhaugh, Carterhaugh,
if you go to Carterhaugh,
Tam Lin'll get you!
Tam Lin's at Carterhaugh,
Tam Lin'll get you!

Janet sits in her high window
   looking out over her father's lands,
a thread of gold in her yellow hair,
   needle and thread in her hand.

'O I'm tired of these grey castle walls!
   I'm tired of sewing seams!
I'd rather be down in Carterhaugh
   among the leaves so green!'

She has thrown her sewing on the chair
   and plaited up her yellow hair,
she's gathered her skirts of green so fair,
   runs lightly down the castle stair
     and away she hies to Carterhaugh
     with a laugh for daring.

*

The wood was quivering with the hum of bees
   and no one she saw

but a milk-white horse by the well under the trees,
    white roses on the briar:
'Some for my room, one for my hair . . .'
but two flowers in her hand – he's there,
sprung up behind her out of thin air,
    saying, 'Lady, you'll pick no more!

'Who said you could pick my roses, Janet,
    or the green branch you've broken?
How dared you come to Carterhaugh
    without my permission?'

'Permission from you, sir? I like that!
    Just who may you be?
I'll go where I please in my own woods
    my father gave to me!'

Tam Lin was no wild robber,
    not foul nor cruel nor grim:
but his face shone with a strange light
for Tam Lin was an elfin knight
    that served the Fairy Queen;
and not her gold but her love he stole,
    and was gone like a dream.

*

'What's come over Janet these days?
    She's changed –'
'She won't play chess,
    she won't come dancing.'

'I've heard her crying in her room!'
'She went to Carterhaugh. I saw –
        ask her, go on.'

'O go away and mind your own business!
        Just leave me alone!'

Her father's coming up the stair:
    'Something's wrong, now tell me, Janet,
are you in trouble? Is it a man?'
        'Father, it's true, I won't deny it.

'And if he were human flesh and blood
    I'd not change him for any man,
but my lover is an elfin knight
        and he'll never ask for my hand.

'But the milk-white horse my true love rides
    is lighter than the wind,
shod with silver shoes before,
        gold shoes behind –'

She has brushed aside her tangled hair,
    taken her cloak of green so rare,
she's left her father standing there,
    runs wildly down the castle stair
        to Carterhaugh, to Carterhaugh,
        eyes red from weeping.

*

The wood was shivering with the fall of leaves
        and no one she saw
but a milk-white horse by the well under the trees,
        the last blooms on the briar:
'Will this bring him back? Will he care?'
but two flowers in her hand – he's there,
sprung up beside her out of thin air,
        saying, 'Lady, you'll pick no more!

'Why are you picking the dead flowers, Janet,
        the dead leaves from the vine?
Are you wanting to harm the unborn baby
        that's your child and mine?'

'O tell me, Tam Lin, tell me,
        if you love me at all,
is it true you're from the other world?
Were you never christened in a church?
        O aren't you real?'

                    *

Tam Lin took her by the hand
        and all the woods grew dim.
'I was born as human a child as you were.
I lived with my grandad Roxburgh
        and I used to ride with him.

'We rode out to hunt the red deer
        with no luck, one day.

Bitter and sharp the wind got up
    and I lost my way.
My horse stumbled on something,
    threw me to the ground,
and so strange a sleep came over me
    I couldn't move or make a sound,
but I could see a tall woman standing there
        as I lay so still:
the Queen of Elfland, come to take me
    to her palace under the hill –

'O Elfland's a fine place to live,
    many stories I could tell,
but at the end of every seven years
    we have to pay a tithe to Hell –
and we pay with one of our people,
    in the fires of Hell to burn,
and because I was once a human lad,
because I'm made of flesh and blood,
    I fear it's my turn.

'But you, if you will, can save me –
    and tonight you may –
you, if you love me, Janet,
        you can win me away.

'Tonight is Halloween, the night
    the fairy people ride:
you must wait for us at Miles Cross
    on the bare hillside.

'Wait there alone at the dead hour
    between twelve hours and one –
cast holy water round where you stand
    and you'll take no harm.'

'Alone with the fairy host, Tam Lin,
    what are you asking me?
To stand in the eye of a nightmare!'
        'To set me free.'

'Alone in the eerie dark, then,
    when they come, if I do,
among all the weird unearthly riders
    how will I ever know which is you?'

'You'll see a black horse: let it pass,
    and after that, a brown –
then run, run to the milk-white steed
    and pull the rider down,
for it's me that's on the milk-white steed –
my right hand gloved, the other bare,
    and one star on my crown.

'Then you must hold on, hold me fast –
    let go once and I'll be lost,
    they'll fight for me with all their powers,
    turn me, I know, to ravening beasts,
        to make you let go.
But never doubt it, what you hold
    is me, the father of your child,
    is me, to be your heart's reward:

and harm you, no, I never would –
   lady, believe it so!

'Last of all
they will turn me to a burning coal
   with flames in your hand:
throw it in the water, love,
   and I'll come out a man –
wrap me then quick in your green cloak, Janet,
   and tomorrow we'll be wed –

'Now we part before they see us –
   Janet, don't be afraid!'

                                    *

Supper's cleared: the lights burn lower,
the shadows twitch and gather and glower,
the corners rustle, the girls are scary:

'Coming up to bed then, Janet?'
   'The wind's like knives!'
'O I hate Halloween, I can't bear to think of it –
   remember last year the ghost on the step?'
'Please yourself, Janet, I'm not staying up.'
      'Goodnight!' *'Goodnight!'*

'Goodnight.'

She has looked in the mirror and said a prayer,
   she's fastened her cloak of green so rare,

crumpled her bed like a body there,
   slipped quietly down the castle stair,
     and she's run off to Miles Cross,
        mouth tight from trembling.

          *

At the dark crossroads all by herself she stands
for the dead of night to call up the cavalcade.
She has sprinkled the holy water with a cold hand –
no moon or stars for her, but the wind like a drawn
            blade –

What was that? What was that? Where?
Far off a faint jang-jangling in the air –
   growing nearer, louder, clearer:
   horses' hooves and horses' bridles,
and over the brow of the hill sweeps down towards her
     the proud host of all the fairy riders.

A black horse passes her, so close,
   so swift, and gone, and now a brown –
and now a white horse, the white horse, his horse, *now*!
She has seized the rider by the foot and pulled him
          down.

   Tam Lin's away! Tam Lin's away!

Is it black night or blinding light?
And what is it twisting in her hands,
that hisses and writhes, with shining fangs?

'I must hold on, he said, he said.'

Hold what in her arms? No speckled snake now,
stifling fur on a form that towers,
with massive paws to overpower –
    'I must hold on, he said, he said.'

But what is she holding? Not a bear,
short hair in her fingers, antlers slashing,
hooves like daggers, kicking, thrashing –
    'I must hold on, he said, he said.'

What must she hold? Not a deer but dead
and heavy and hard and harsh as iron
but red-hot, a bar of red-hot iron –
    'I must hold on, he said, he said.'

And now in her hand? No weight, no raging –
like an egg, like a stone, with a flame that flickers –
like a coal from a fire that cannot burn her:
    'Tam Lin, I'll win!' she said, she said.

She has thrown the coal into the well water.
The shape of a man she has covered over.
    What now the terrors of the night?
He is under her green mantle, wrapped tight.

*

Out then spoke the Fairy Queen,
    out of a bush of broom:

'Whoever's won my young Tam Lin
    has won a noble groom.

'But shame on her ill-fared human face
    and an ill death may she die,
for stealing the best and bonniest knight
    of all my company!

'O had I known this morning
    Tam Lin would be gone,
I'd have taken out his heart of flesh
    and left him a heart of stone.

'The look he had this evening
    O if I'd understood,
I'd have taken out his two grey eyes.
    I'd have given him eyes of wood.

'And had I learned last night, Tam Lin,
    what I've learned this hour,
seven tithes I'd have paid to Hell
    before I let you go!'

*

The Queen of Elfland cursed and cried,
    but her rage was vain.
Janet stood fast at Miles Cross
    and she married Tam Lin.

Libby Houston

The Faery Earl

Oh, who is this comes ridin',
   Ridin' down the glen?
Is it one of our own Red-Branch Knights
   Or one of the King's men?

With feathers on his helmet,
   And gold upon his shield,
His horse is shod with silver shoes,
   He's ridin' through the field!

Oh, this is not a Red-Branch
   Nor one of the King's men,
But this is faery Desmond
   Come ridin' back again.

'O lady of the Castle,
   O lady with gold hair,
O lady with eyes of pity,
   Come down the grey tower stair.

'For I may ask a question,
   And you may answer me,
When the sun is red in the forest,
   And the moon is white on the sea.'

Says she, 'Sir, ask your question,
   And I will answer you;

At sunset or at moonrise
  God send that I speak true!

'I know you by your helmet,
  And by your voice so sweet,
And by your coal-black charger
  With silver on his feet.

'God send you, faery Desmond,
  To come back to your own.'
Says he, 'Your answer, lady,
  Before the sun goes down.

'I'm ridin' ever and ever
  Over the land and sea;
My horse's shoes of silver,
  How long will they last me?'

The lady stood and pondered,
  The salt tear in her eye –
'Oh, would that I had magic
  To make a wise reply.

'Oh, will they wear forever,
  Or will they wear out fast?
Will he ride home this even'
  And stable his horse at last?'

'Sweet lady, quick, your answer!'
  'Now, God, what can I say? –

Those silver shoes will last, sir,
  To ride till Judgement Day.'

He turned, that faery horseman,
  And shook his bridle rein;
'Now, come the Day of Judgement
  Ere I ride home again.'

The sun went down in the forest,
  The moon shone bright as pearl,
The lady lay in the castle,
  And died for the faery Earl.

And ye will see him ridin',
  Ridin' down the glen
Over the seas and rivers,
  Over the hill and the plain.

Ye'll see the plume on his helmet
  Waftin' among the trees,
And the silver shoes of his charger
  Chasin' the moonlit seas.

He's ridin' ever and ever,
  He'll ride till Judgement Day;
Oh, when that ride is over,
  May he ride home, we pray!

                    Rosa Mulholland

The Fairies

Up the airy mountain,
    Down the rushy glen,
We daren't go a-hunting
    For fear of little men;
Wee folk, good folk,
    Trooping all together;
Green jacket, red cap,
    And white owl's feather!

Down along the rocky shore
    Some make their home,
They live on crispy pancakes
    Of yellow tide-foam;
Some in the reeds
    Of the black mountain-lake,
With frogs for their watchdogs,
    All night awake.

High on the hill-top
    The old King sits;
He is now so old and grey
    He's nigh lost his wits.
With a bridge of white mist
    Columbkill he crosses,
On his stately journeys
    From Slieveleague to Rosses;
Or going up with music

On cold starry nights,
To sup with the Queen
Of the gay Northern Lights.

They stole little Bridget
For seven years long;
When she came down again
Her friends were all gone.
They took her lightly back,
Between the night and morrow,
They thought that she was fast asleep,
But she was dead with sorrow.
They have kept her ever since
Deep within the lake,
On a bed of flag-leaves,
Watching till she wake.

By the craggy hill-side,
Through the mosses bare,
They have planted thorn trees
For pleasure, here and there.
Is any man so daring
As dig them up in spite,
He shall find their sharpest thorns
In his bed at night.

Up the airy mountains,
Down the rushy glen,
We daren't go a-hunting
For fear of little men;

Wee folk, good folk,
  Trooping all together;
Green jacket, red cap,
  And white owl's feather!

William Allingham

Fairies

There are fairies at the bottom of our garden!
    It's not so very, very far away;
You pass the gardener's shed and you just keep
                               straight ahead –
    I do so hope they've really come to stay.
There's a little wood, with moss in it and beetles,
    And a little stream that quietly runs through;
You wouldn't think they'd dare to come merrymaking
                                   there –
      Well, they do.

There are fairies at the bottom of our garden!
    They often have a dance on summer nights;
The butterflies and bees make a lovely little breeze,
    And the rabbits stand about and hold the lights.
Did you know that they could sit upon the
                                  moonbeams
    And pick a little star to make a fan,
And dance away up there in the middle of the air?
      Well, they can.

There are fairies at the bottom of our garden!
    You cannot think how beautiful they are;
They all stand up and sing when the Fairy Queen and
                                    King
    Come gently floating down upon their car.

The King is very proud and *very* handsome;
    The Queen – now can you guess who that could be
(She's a little girl all day, but at night she steals

                       away)?

    Well – it's ME!

                           Rose Fyleman

A Fairy Went A-Marketing

A fairy went a-marketing –
　　She bought a little fish;
She put it in a crystal bowl
　　Upon a golden dish.
An hour she sat in wonderment
　　And watched its silver gleam,
And then she gently took it up
　　And slipped it in a stream.

A fairy went a-marketing –
　　She bought a coloured bird;
It sang the sweetest, shrillest song
　　That ever she had heard.
She sat beside its painted cage
　　And listened half the day,
And then she opened wide the door
　　And let it fly away.

A fairy went a-marketing –
She bought a winter gown
All stitched about with gossamer
　　And lined with thistledown.
She wore it all the afternoon
　　With prancing and delight,
Then gave it to a little frog
　　To keep him warm at night.

A fairy went a-marketing –
  She bought a gentle mouse
To take her tiny messages,
  To keep her tiny house.
All day she kept its busy feet
  Pit-patting to and fro,
And then she kissed its silken ears,
  Thanked it, and let it go.

Rose Fyleman

Instructions for Spotting and Trapping a Fairy

(for Stevie)

Go to Cuckoo Wood after sunset on Mid Never's Eve.
It is there you will have a good view of fairy folk
as they play, flit and dance under summer's few stars.

Arm yourself with these items of equipment:
a silvery bag made from spiders' webs;
a golden leaf with the name of a fairy written upon
    it;
a sip of polished water carried in your hand.

At Cuckoo Wood, hide the bag in a bird's nest.
Bury the leaf under a young tree.
Pour the polished water into a dark pond.
Leave without looking back, taking nothing.

Return to Cuckoo Wood a year and a day later
(but not if it is a Thursday).
The spider-web bag will have decayed,
the leaf will have rotted,
and the water will have dissolved.

You will find your fairy fast asleep in the nest.

It is then that you will discover the bag has trapped
the fairy's lustre and sweet personality;

that the leaf has absorbed the fairy's language
and that the water reflects the fairy's beauty.

Transport your fairy to a long, narrow garden
that has an Old Man's Bench facing south.

Now, amidst the blare of daffodil trumpets,
the din of a pack of cats singing in Old Irish
and the clamour of gushing water features,
set your fairy free. Let fly!

And if there is an old man on the bench
at that particular moment, he will welcome
the fairy and befriend it.
Do not be surprised if, together, they leave –
amidst prickly sun and biting moon,
taking new names – Mischief and Eternity –
to become homely in some other kingdom.

And you,
you yourself you,
you will hear an entrancing new music,
a bow drawn slow over a warm violin,
a feathered piano in a summery rose room,

all times the mischievous fairies visit you,
and visit you they will.

John Rice

If You Were a Fairy ...

If YOU were a fairy
What would you wear?

A circle of raindrops to shine in your hair?
A bangle of blossoms? A necklace of ice?
Spider-silk dresses embroidered by mice?
A fluttery nightgown with holes for your wings?
A daisy-chain scarf and some morning-star rings?
Or a fiery crown that would flicker and flare?

If you were a fairy
What would YOU wear?

If YOU were a fairy,
Where would you fly?

To woods where the unicorns wander and cry?
To caves where the dragons lie sleepily curled?
To waves where the mermaids are happily swirled?
To castles that grow from the glistening sands?
To magical mountains? To looking-glass lands?
To a city of clouds in the blue summer sky?

If you were a fairy,
Where would YOU fly?

Clare Bevan

45

The Chime Child

The Chime Child was born
When the clock struck three,
She was odder than plums
On an apple tree.

She listened to secrets
That swirled in her head,
She spoke to the shadows
That circled her bed.

And the songs that she sang
Were so sad and so sweet
The fairies came dancing
Around her feet.

Clare Bevan

*Chime Children are born when the clock strikes
three, six, nine or twelve, and some stories
say they can see the fairies.*

Fairytale

Nobody quite believed it –
a briar hedge,
tangle-twisted and thorn-sharp,
holding in its core a secret
fragile as blossom
drifting on a springtime breeze.

And yet the story lingered –
whispered softly
by winter firesides,
a story of enchantment
and a sleeping world,
a dreaming princess
chained within a fairy spell.

Only the golden prince believed –
he heard the story,
heard the sighs
and with his valiant sword
hacked down the tangled hedge
to find his princess
wrapped in cobwebbed dreams.

Gentle as gossamer
his soft lips touched her cheek.
Who could resist the kiss
of such a prince,
the sweet awakening
to a fairytale romance?

Cynthia Rider

Haiku

Mushrooms in a ring,
fluttering gossamer wings:
fairy folk gather.

Debjani Chatterjee

Fairies in the Garden

Fairies flying sideways,
　blown in the breeze,
Fairies in the foxgloves,
　dancing with the bees,
Fairies in the treetops,
　polishing the nuts,
Fairies falling sleepy
　as the daisy petal shuts.

Fairies in the springtime,
　dewdrops in their hair,
Fairies in the summer
　with daisy chains to spare,
Fairies in the autumn,
　in gowns of golden fronds,
Fairies in the winter
　with snowflake wands.

Celia Warren

Faerie

They are dark,
The secret ones,
The old ones
Who live at the edges
Where day meets night
And where dreams merge
With waking thought.

They are dangerous
And in their company
We become the lost,
The wandering ones
Who have forgotten home.

Time moves round them
Like whispering silk,
But does not touch them.
They come and go
Are every-when
And where.

They offer gifts. Fakes. Tricks.
They tempt. Promise. Lie.
So stay, stay,
Do not follow the glint of silver
In the darkening sky.

Do not listen to their golden songs –
   Swan's-feather-in-sunset songs –
They sing.
How can they love us?
How can they love our life,
Those that do not die?

Jan Dean

A Gift from the Fairies

The lawn is sprinkled with daisies,
the fairies' gift to those who mourn
the passing of a child.

White, bright-eyed,
they open up
their petals to the sun.

My daughter sits on the lawn
making daisy chains;
wreaths of innocence and joy,
crowns for fairies.

Patricia Leighton

How Beautiful They Are

How beautiful they are, the lordly ones
Who dwell in the hills
In the hollow hills.
They have faces like flowers
And their breath is wind that stirs amid the grasses
Filled with white clover.
Their limbs are more white than shafts of moonshine.
They are more fleet than the March wind.
They laugh and are glad and are terrible:
When their lances shake, every green reed quivers.
How beautiful they are
How beautiful the lordly ones
In the hollow hills.

Fiona MacLeod

Fiona MacLeod is the pseudonym
of William Sharp (1855–1905)

The Girl Who Could See Fairies

Wings whispered about her hair
as she walked, half in the Otherworld,
half in the mortal realm.
She saw massive oaks
dwarfing the grimy buildings,
overlaying them like great, dark ghosts.
She glimpsed, with her double vision,
a white stag leaping through the passing traffic
and felt a wreath of berries placed lightly on her
    head.
Bluebells burst through the pavement beneath her
    feet
and she trod through them as if in a dream.
Nobody believed that she could see fairies.
She was mocked
and eventually, locked
into a hospital room
from where, one day,
she stepped out of the mortal world
and into the Otherworld,
leaving the room empty
but for the scent of forests.

Marian Swinger

A Fairy's Revenge

I saw a fairy flitting
through the scented summer flowers,
slipping past the roses
and the blue delphinium towers.

She fluttered with the butterflies,
buzzed around the bees,
bounced upon a sunflower,
then wafted on the breeze.

It was then I tried to catch her
but she produced a tiny wand
and now I'm just a little frog
croaking in a pond.

Marian Swinger

Faery Flights

(Faery Folk on the Island of Barra)

By night but not by day
they wheeled and darted around my bedroom.
Those tiny balls of light –
blue, green, yellow, red
and colours I did not know the names of.

They were neither souls nor spirits,
just the tail lights of the Faeries
busy on what looked like pointless errands.

Surrounded by an ocean of night silence,
I could hear their little voices singing work
  songs.
From time to time they rattled tiny keys
as they circled above the old sea chest
that sat under the window sill.

One of these nights the fog came.
I heard one Faery Woman say,
'It is early today that I have risen.'
And another replied, 'Tomorrow I shall rise at
  daybreak.'

I, too, rose at daybreak to watch
the Faeries raise their own kind's flag
on the beach where sand meets water.

And just as the slow tide began to ebb,
so the Faery Women disappeared into
the only cloud that was in the sky that morning.

If I am to see them again,
I shall have to visit the island once more
and wait for the fiery cauldron of sunset.

John Rice

The Fairies Have Never a Penny to Spend

The fairies have never a penny to spend,
   They haven't a thing put by,
But theirs is the dower of bird and of flower
   And theirs are the earth and the sky.
And though you should live in a palace of gold
   Or sleep in a dried-up ditch,
You could never be poor as the fairies are,
     And never as rich.

Since ever and ever the world began
   They have danced like a ribbon of flame,
They have sung their song through the centuries long
   And yet it is never the same.
And though you be foolish or though you be wise,
   With hair of silver or gold,
You could never be young as the fairies are,
     And never as old.

Rose Fyleman

One-Wing

One-Wing was different,
Yet she didn't seem to mind.

When the Fairy Queen (with a sad smile)
Promised to weave a rare and dazzling spell
From the feather of a flying horse,
The sparkle of the stars,
And the blue of the evening sky,
The fairy-child just laughed and said:

'But then I would not be
One-Wing.
I would be as ordinary
As a green leaf
Or a dull grey cloud.'

Then she jumped on the back
Of the giant jackdaw
Who called her his little jewel,
And they swooped away
To play with the summer swallows.

Clare Bevan

Fairy Song

Who shoos the sulky rain away,
Puts rainbows in the sky?

Who melts dangling icicles,
Calms gales which terrify?

Who propels the comets
That streak across the night?

Who makes the stars come out
And keeps them shining bright?

Who wakes up the daisies
To sing songs to the sun?

Who even puts the currants
Inside a currant bun?

Or the fizz in fizzy lemonade
And juice inside a berry?

Who makes sure the colour's right
On orange, plum or cherry?

Who fixes the way the tide
Makes furrows in the sand?

What would you do,
What would you do without us,
The folk of fairyland?

Matt Simpson

Tooth Fairy

Put your lost tooth
under the pillow.
Go to sleep
and keep quite still
so in the morning
when you wake
there'll be a coin
for you to take.

Jill Townsend

The Kelpie of Loch Coruisk

In the morning, a milky sun
peeks over the spear-tips of the mountain.
Two infant clouds chase each other
across an ocean of sky.

This is the kind of day that
the Kelpie of Loch Coruisk loves.
A green sea-wind on his snowdrop-white blaze,
a warm sun on his rock-black back.

The wash and whine of the sea is his orchestra:
the gulls, the seals, the gannets
unite in song to become his choir.
And on a slab of sparkling rock, he dances.

This is no jittering Scottish jig, no rushing Irish reel.
This is a fast-flowing, watery wave of a dance –
a hoof-to-the-heavens swirling, swishing, sweeping
surge of a dance, a defiant devil of a dance!

Ho, there's no stopping him! He's off across
the loch's cold water, full speed down the glen,
skimming the rocky scree, disappearing over
the sharpest peak in a sound like cracking wood.

This is the kind of day that
the Kelpie of Loch Coruisk loves.
A day when dancing can be fun and joyful.
A day when he gets time off from drowning people.

John Rice

Fairy Picnic

Under our kitchen table
on the new carpet
the fairies have prepared a picnic –
tiny little cookies,
funny little cakes,
weeny little biscuits,
scrummy fairy flakes,
sarnies small as bee eyes,
pretty little buns.
It's called a fairy picnic . . .
but Mum says it's just crumbs.

Peter Dixon

The Village Changeling

Rose held her sleepy first-born tight,
She kissed him once and twice,
'God knows I wouldn't swap,' she said,
'My child for any price.'

But in the night the Fairies came
And stole her son away,
And in his place she found instead
A Changeling Child, they say.

And though the crooked creature squealed
Like rabbits in a snare,
Rose hugged it to her broken heart
And stroked its tangled hair.

'For if I hold you safe,' she sighed,
'Through sickness and through storm,
Perhaps the Fairy Folk will keep
My own lost child from harm.'

All year, the Changeling wailed for home,
Its eyes grew blank and wide,
While Rose, in pity, kissed its hands
And shivered when it died.

Their grave lies in a hidden place
Yet still, the story goes,
A sleepy boy will sometimes come
To leave a wild, white rose.

Clare Bevan

The Fairy and the Foxglove

A tiny little fairy,
So the stories tell,
Once found a dying foxglove
With just one withered bell.

The fairy kissed it gently
And tended it each day,
And soon, instead of one bell
A host came out to play.

And that one little fairy,
The story fondly tells,
Is the reason why all foxgloves
Are full of fairy bells.

Clive Webster

The Stolen Child

Where dips the rocky highland
Of Sleuth Wood in the lake,
There lies a leafy island
Where flapping herons wake
The drowsy water rats;
There we've hid our faery vats,
Full of berries
And of reddest stolen cherries.
Come away, O human child!
To the waters and the wild
With a faery, hand in hand,
For the world's more full of weeping than
you can understand.

Where the wave of moonlight glosses
The dim grey sands with light,
Far off by furthest Rosses
We foot it all the night,
Weaving olden dances,
Mingling hands and mingling glances
Till the moon has taken flight;
To and fro we leap
And chase the frothy bubbles,
While the world is full of troubles
And is anxious in its sleep.
Come away, O human child!
To the waters and the wild

With a faery, hand in hand,
For the world's more full of weeping than
                    you can understand.

Where the wandering water gushes
From the hills above Glen-Car,
In pools among the rushes
That scarce could bathe a star,
We seek for slumbering trout
And whispering in their ears
Give them unquiet dreams;
Leaning softly out
From ferns that drop their tears
Over the young streams.
Come away, O human child!
To the waters and the wild
With a faery, hand in hand,
For the world's more full of weeping than
                    you can understand.

Away with us he's going,
The solemn-eyed:
He'll hear no more the lowing
Of the calves on the warm hillside
Or the kettle on the hob
Sing peace into his breast,
Or see the brown mice bob
Round and round the oatmeal-chest.

For he comes, the human child,
To the waters and the wild
With a faery, hand in hand,
From a world more full of weeping than
                    he can understand.

                              W. B. Yeats

The cauldron of sunset

Beyond the horizon
(itself a rhythmic alignment
of seal-silver, gull-gold),
the Atlantic is poised for the moment of sunset;
a fluent blue cruet waiting for
that final drip of honey sun.

And the sand,
and the sand,
and the sand,
o the sand is the several colours
of a Fairy shoemaker's apron.

                              John Rice

The Enchanted Island

To Rathlin's Isle I chanced to sail,
  When summer breezes softly blew,
And there I heard so sweet a tale,
  That oft I wished it could be true.
They said, at eve, when rude winds sleep,
  And hushed is every turbid swell,
A mermaid rises from the deep,
  And sweetly tunes her magic shell.

And while she plays, rock, dell and cave,
  In dying falls the sound retain,
As if some choral spirits gave
  Their aid to swell her witching strain.
Then summoned by that dulcet note,
  Uprising to th' admiring view,
A fairy island seems to float
  With tints of many a gorgeous hue.

And glittering fanes, and lofty towers,
  All on this fairy isle are seen;
And waving trees, and shady bowers,
  With more than mortal verdure green.
And as it moves, the western sky
  Glows with a thousand varying rays;
And the calm sea, tinged with each dye,
  Seems like a golden flood of blaze.

They also say, if earth or stone,
  From verdant Erin's hallowed land,
Were on this magic island thrown,
  Forever fixed, it then would stand.
But when, for this, some little boat
  In silence ventures from the shore –
The mermaid sinks – hushed is the note,
  The fairy isle is seen no more!

Anon.

On Midsummer Night

A lone reveller,
Violin case under one arm,
Is off away home
And his path is well lit
By a new-birthed full moon.

Now mind and eyes grow weary
When a path is straight and narrow
So yawning, he takes a short cut
Past the Fairy Rath
That's covered in clover
Just like an ancient barrow.

Now the clover's soft
And the night air's sweet
So he stretches out
And is soon fast asleep:
You might say
He is far from sober.

While he snorts
And he snores
And he sings in his sleep,
A door opens up in the Rath,
Out pour the fairies,
Silent as snowfall,
And each one has eyes like a cat.

Gently they carry him
In through the door,
Down a long tunnel
And into their Hall
Where they pinch him awake
With 'Give us a reel!'
So he opens the case,
Gets out his fiddle
And plays them
A river with meltwater swollen,
Crashing and tumbling down a hillside,
The madness of poets and wild birds in flight.

At his pause, they're all gasping
And drink deep of their wine
And now he is playing faster again
So they dance and they jig
In wild spinning reels
And each time he pauses,
Drink deeper again.

Full seven times
Does he pause while they drink,
At the eighth, now quite senseless,
To the ground they all sink.

Now scattered around
Are crocks full of gold
And he fills his pockets,
His cap and his boots,

He's rich as a Lord now
But it's still not enough
So he slings his old fiddle
And fills the case up.
While the fairies are stirring
And starting to wake,
He grabs the plunder
And makes his escape.
As their door slams shut behind him,
Dawn starts to break.

Well he's dancing for joy
And his ill-gotten gains
But when he empties his pockets,
His boots and his cap,
There's nothing but gravel
And in his violin case
The tale's just the same.
Well now he's left cursing
His greed and his thieving
And for his lost fiddle
Is inconsolably grieving,
So he gets a lift home
On some old tinker's cart
But now he never makes music:
He hasn't the heart.

Kevin McCann

A Fairy Rath (or Forth) is a small rounded hill.
Never go to sleep on one.

72

To Stay on the Good Side of Fairies . . .

Don't throw dirty water
On to any path at sunset,
Don't trample flowers
Or damage trees,
Don't kill ants, birds or
Hedgehogs, in fact,
Don't ever hurt any living thing.

Never curse a beggar
Or be cruel to strangers.

They are almost always
Not what they seem.

If you get lost
In a familiar place,
Turn your coat inside out
And don't try to outwit them:
You'll only end up
With an old donkey's head.

Kevin McCann

73

Dance of Death

Look, look, 'tis Will o' the Wisp
Beckoning, beckoning out of the mist

See his light flicker
Flutter and prance
Calling lost mortals
To join in the dance.

Here he darts, there he darts
Now softly glows
Fuddling men's senses
With magical shows.

Spirit of marshland
Moorland and bog
Like moths to a candle flame
Will lures them on.

Lures them and leaves them
To sink out of sight
Grasping at shadows
Tricked by the light

Of Will, Will, Will o' the Wisp
Beckoning, beckoning out of the mist

Patricia Leighton

A Far Journey

Hobgoblin, hobgoblin,
where are you going?
Over the mountain
so cold and so stark.

Hobgoblin, hobgoblin,
why are you going
over the mountain
so cold and so stark?

To find a green valley
of flowers and bright butterflies,
flowers and bright butterflies,
cherries and pears.

Hobgoblin, hobgoblin,
what will you do there,
what will you do
in that valley so fair?

I shall find me a home
beneath an old willow,
beneath an old willow
beside a slow stream.

And who will live with you
beneath the old willow,
who will live with you
beside the slow stream?

No one, no one.
What will you do then?
Weep and sing
Weep and sing.

Patricia Leighton

Leanan-Sidhe

Only half-aware at first,
He sifted phrases,
Stones sized and chosen
For their shape,
Their polished lustre.

She was
A murmur on his page,
Elusive,
A rising breeze.

She became
His eyes and ears,
Let him assume
The transparent ease
Of a blind man
Playing Knucklebones.

Kevin McCann

*Pronounced Lan-awn-shee, she is a
solitary fairy and the inspiration of poets.*

What I Saw from My Window One Mayday Morning

There was a movement in the grass,
Then, drawn by twenty ladybirds,
I saw Queen Silva's chariot pass.

Twenty-five elves marched on ahead,
Blowing on tiny silver trumpets;
Their suits were green, their caps were red.

Flying about her was a crew
Of waiting-maids with rainbow wings,
Who sang a sweet song as they flew.

And at her back, four goblins true
Carried a table with a feast
Of berries, roasted nuts and dew.

Then, as they reached my garden pond,
Quite suddenly the music changed;
Queen Silva waved her fairy wand

And up they rose, that fairy crew,
And shimmered in the morning air
As swift across the pond they flew.

I gazed upon them while I could,
Until they dipped and disappeared
Into Tom Darley's bluebell wood.

Gerard Benson

Winter Window

Frosted fairies, powder-light,
feathered their tiny wings, last night,
across my winter window,

carved a crystal paradise
of snowflake patterns and bracken in ice
across my winter window,

blew cold, rolling scrolls and curls
that froze to etch an Arctic world
across my winter window.

Gina Douthwaite

La Belle Dame Sans Merci

'O what can ail thee, Knight-at-arms,
Alone and palely loitering?
The sedge is wither'd from the lake,
And no birds sing.

'O what can ail thee, Knight-at-arms,
So haggard and so woebegone?
The squirrel's granary is full,
And the harvest's done.

'I see a lily on thy brow
With anguish moist and fever dew,
And on thy cheek a fading rose
Fast withereth too.'

'I met a lady in the meads
Full beautiful – a faery's child,
Her hair was long, her foot was light,
And her eyes were wild.

'I made a garland for her head,
And bracelets too, and fragrant zone;
She look'd at me as she did love,
And made sweet moan.

'I set her on my pacing steed,
And nothing else saw all day long,
For sidelong would she bend and sing
A faery's song.

'She found me roots of relish sweet,
And honey wild and manna dew,
And sure in language strange she said,
"I love thee true."

'She took me to her elfin grot,
And there she wept and sigh'd full sore;
And there I shut her wild wild eyes
With kisses four.

'And there she lulled me asleep,
And there I dream'd – Ah! woe betide!
The latest dream I ever dream'd
On the cold hill's side.

'I saw pale kings and princes too,
Pale warriors, death-pale were they all:
Who cried – "La Belle Dame sans Merci
Hath thee in thrall!"

'I saw their starv'd lips in the gloam
With horrid warning gaped wide,
And I awoke and found me here
On the cold hill's side.

'And this is why I sojourn here
Alone and palely loitering,
Though the sedge is wither'd from the lake,
And no birds sing.'

John Keats

How to Find Your Fairy Name

On my fairy naming day
I was christened Wings-of-Gauze.
You can find your name this way –
Light a sparkler out of doors,
Let it guide your hand and write
On the blackboard of the night.

Sue Cowling

Faery Song

Shed no tear – O shed no tear!
The flower will bloom another year.
Weep no more – O weep no more!
Young buds sleep in the root's white core.
Dry your eyes – O dry your eyes!
For I was taught in Paradise
To ease my breast of melodies –
        Shed no tear.

Overhead – Look overhead
'Mong the blossoms white and red –
Look up, look up. I flutter now
On this flush pomegranate bough –
See me – 'tis this silvery bill
Ever cures the good man's ill –
Shed no tear – O shed no tear!
The flower will bloom another year.
Adieu, adieu – I fly, adieu!
I vanish in the heaven's blue –
        Adieu, Adieu!

John Keats

Hee-Haw

This wood is full of magic –
fairy tunes stop spotted snakes from hissing,
moth and cobweb drift a hammock
for Titania's bed – and I
sing braying songs to warn of day's approach.

But even I was amazed, silenced
when the master's boy
took my noble head and fixed it
on that idiot weaver's neck.

I felt a garland of oxlips and wild thyme
twined all about my ears,
the whisper of fairy fingers through my fur:
looked down to see
a gross and ugly body wrapped
in hemp and homespun.

I could hear
the queen's rich promises of love
fill silky channels of my mind,
spiced with the snap of mustardseed.

I guessed the master would put it right,
clip Robin's ear, bring balance
to the chaos started by that changeling boy.
I never thought
how much the changing back would hurt,
how sharp my anguished bray would sound.

Was it a dream? I'm standing here,
head square on shoulders, my back's cross-aligned.
Stamping jolts familiar vibrations,
makes my skull ring as it always did.

But I have been transformed,
have learned frail back, weak shoulder,
know how mortals buckle under love,
know I can never forget.

Alison Chisholm

Twilight Wind

There's a wind here and a wind there, there's the mad
old wind from the sea,
The dancing breeze of the morning hours, and the
storm wind, fierce and shrill;
But there's nothing so sweet in all the world as the
wind that cries to me
When the sun is low and the tide is low and I climb
along our hill.

'Tis the twilight wind, the enchanted wind, and it
sings a magical rune,
And all the whishty people wake as it wanders up
and down,
Strumming its queer little shadowy fiddle beneath the
light of the moon,
In a mist of sunset and dusk and the chimney smoke
of the dreaming town.

I climb along the dew-set lane, and I listen among
the trees,
And watch the wee little elfin folk lighting their tiny
fires,
The teeny-weeny shoemaker men are working as hard
as you please,
And the darling fairy babies are swinging high in the
foxglove spires.

The dancers dance in the fairy ring to the throb of
                                    fiddle and fife,
While the magic song of the twilight wind beats out
                                    the lilting time;
The cobweb threads are gathered and spun by each
                                    little brisk good-wife,
While the crooked goblin ringers o' bells are playing
                                    a fairy chime.

Now don't you hearken to folk as say that the night
                                    is darksome and chill;
Just you follow the twilight wind as it flees along the
                                    hill,
And you meet the Little Good Folk up there, many a
                                    time and again.

Thora Stowell

St George's Day Rhyme

Don't go into the woods alone
Wearing a dress of blue.
Don't go picking the fairy flowers –
Someone is watching you!

Where's the little sister
Who wandered off to play?
The fairy folk, the fairy folk
Have stolen her away!

Don't be seen on St George's Day
With bluebells in your hand.
Don't get caught by the fairies
Or you're off to fairyland!

Where's the little sister
Who wandered off to play?
The fairy folk, the fairy folk
Have stolen her away!

Sue Cowling

Bedtime Fairies

Fleeting glimpses hard to find,
Imagined wonders of lovely kind.
In night times waking in pleasant dreams,
In the moon's gossamer, silver beams.
Fairies dance the night away,
Gone at dawn in flight of day.

L. C. Gerstenfeld

CobWebs

Between me and the rising sun,
This way and that the cobwebs run;
Their myriad wavering lines of light
Dance up the hill and out of sight.

There is no land possesses half
So many lines of telegraph
As those the spider-elves have spun
Between me and the rising sun.

E. L. King

Robin Goodfellow

Where are you,
    Old Shape-shifter?
Come down from that apple tree
Where I can see you!
Lead me astray would you,
    Brat of a scullery-maid?
Did she teach you
To sweep dust in eyes,
    Prize a fool,
Serve misrule?
Come on, you phantom stool-lifter,
Down here to me
    My Hob
    My Robin Roundcap!
Come and dance with me,
    Sweep me, leap me,
    Take me away . . .
Come down, I say!

David Orme

Finding a Fairy

The woods are full of them.

You just need to know
when and where
they are.

Try dusk.

Just at the moment
when the sun dies
and the dark falls
you'll find them
hovering
in the shadows
darting
in between
the trunks of trees.

What? Was that one there?
Of course it was.
Trust me.

But don't follow.
You're wasting your time.
Moreover, if one
catches you –
say a night fairy –

it can be bad news.

Keep looking.

The woods are full of them.

James Carter

Scottish Charm

From every brownie and banshee,
From every evil wish and sorrow,
From every nymph and water-wraith,
From every fairy-mouse and grass-mouse
. . . Oh, save me to the end of my day.

Trad

Indian Fairies

Whirling fairies spin and turn,
their scarlet sarees swirling,
while wands of gold and silver
in nimble hands are twirling.

Twinkling fairies sweetly chant
old songs in Hindustani
as with jasmine chains they crown
their Raja and their Rani.

They live in their starry realm,
but on moonlit nights they fly
to jackfruit and mango groves
in bright clusters in the sky.

Indian fairies jingle
their anklets, bracelets and rings
to music, dance and laughter,
as they soar on silken wings.

Debjani Chatterjee

The Fairies' Lament

No more shall we dance round the King Stone,
no more shall we sing the old songs.
Since they hung loud bells in the church
we're disturbed by the hourly ding-dongs.

There's no rest for us here any more,
we're sleepless and awful distressed,
since they dressed the bells at Easter time,
since the bells in the tower were blessed.

So we're packing up now and we're moving,
far away from this noisy hill,
far away from these wretched chimes
that are making us sour and ill.

And the first stroke of midnight will find us
leaving the sacred oak,
no more will be heard on this hillside
the chatter of fairy folk.

Our mood may be lifted elsewhere,
our hearts may be lighter too,
and the tunes we play on our pipes,
the bells will no longer subdue.

Somewhere else on full-moon nights
we can sing without disruption,
no ding-dongs then to annoy us
with their constant interruption.

And what will remain, you may ask,
of the fairies who dwelt for so long?
On the breeze, at the end of the day, perhaps
a snatch of a fairy song.

Brian Moses

*This is a story of fairies who left their
homes because of noisy church bells.*

We Wait

We wait
hang in the air
just out of reach
until you think us
into a shape.

Sometimes you see wings
and then we fly
part angel, part insect,
born of flowers and longing.

Or else it's wind and weather
– then we gleam
with yellow eyes of livid skies
or prowl
grey as fog
and treacherous.

Your minds make us
both gossamer and fanged.
But the who and why and what of us
is not for you to know.
We come.
We go.

Jan Dean

The Old Man's Wishes

A fairy went North, South, East and West
doing the things a fairy does best.
She found an old man who lived in a drain, she
    heard him complain,
'It's a shame, it's a shame, it's a shame,
I shouldn't live in this stinky drain but in a wooden
    hut.'
'Very well,' the fairy said,
'turn three times round when you go to bed
and in the morning you'll see what you'll see.'
So the old man did as the fairy said
he turned three times round when he went to bed
and in the morning he woke to see
he was in a wooden hut.
And he was so pleased as pleased could be,
he forgot to thank the fairy.

Then the fairy went North, South, East and West
doing the things a fairy does best.
When she came back to see how the old man was,
    she heard him complain,
'It's a shame, it's a shame, it's a shame,
I shouldn't live in this wooden hut but in a little
    cottage.'
'Very well,' the fairy said,
'turn three times round when you go to bed
and in the morning you'll see what you'll see.'

So the old man did as the fairy said
he turned three times round when he went to bed
and in the morning he woke to see
he was in a little cottage.
And he was so pleased as pleased could be,
he forgot to thank the fairy.

Then the fairy went North, South, East and West
doing the things a fairy does best.
When she came back to see how the old man was,
  she heard him complain,
'It's a shame, it's a shame, it's a shame,
I shouldn't live in a little cottage but in a proper
  brick house.'
'Very well,' the fairy said,
'turn three times round when you go to bed
and in the morning you'll see what you'll see.'
So the old man did as the fairy said
he turned three times round when he went to bed
and in the morning he woke to see
he was in a proper brick house.
And he was so pleased as pleased could be,
he forgot to thank the fairy.

Then the fairy went North, South, East and West
doing the things a fairy does best.
When she came back to see how the old man was,
  she heard him complain,
'It's a shame, it's a shame, it's a shame,
I shouldn't live in a brick house but in a stone villa.'

'Very well,' the fairy said,
'turn three times round when you go to bed
and in the morning you'll see what you'll see.'
So the old man did as the fairy said
he turned three times round when he went to bed
and in the morning he woke to see
he was in a smart stone villa.
And he was so pleased as pleased could be,
he forgot to thank the fairy.

Then the fairy went North, South, East and West
doing the things a fairy does best.
When she came back to see how the old man was,
    she heard him complain,
'It's a shame, it's a shame, it's a shame,
I shouldn't live in a villa but in a marble palace.'
'Very well,' the fairy said,
'turn three times round when you go to bed
and in the morning you'll see what you'll see.'
So the old man did as the fairy said
he turned three times round when he went to bed
and in the morning he woke to see
he was back in the drain.

Dave Calder

Who Believes in Fairies?

No one believes in fairies now,
tiny flittery things
with see-through wings.
No one believes they are true.
I don't. Do you?

Well – sometimes –
on the summer nights
when the patio door is open
and the breeze makes strange
noises among the trees;
when the stars glitter
and silver moonshine
sparkles and flashes
between the leaves;
when our dog on the lawn
sits dead still
and stares, just stares,
at thin air – well –
I do wonder.

Patricia Leighton

Index of First Lines

Acknowledgements

The publisher would like to thank the following for permission to use copyright material:

Benson, Catherine: 'Somewhere in the World' by permission of the author; Benson, Gerard: 'The Water Sprites' and 'What I Saw from My Window One Mayday Morning' by permission of the author; Bevan, Clare: 'Fairy Names' first published in *Fairy Poems*, Macmillan Children's Books (2004), 'If You Were a Fairy', 'One-Wing', 'The Village Changeling' and 'The Chime Child' all by permission of the author; Calder, Dave: 'The Old Man's Wishes' copyright © 2006 by permission of the author; Chatterjee, Debjani: 'Haiku' and 'Indian Fairies' by permission of the author; Chisholm, Alison: 'Midnight Fairy' and 'Hee-Haw' by permission of the author; Cowling, Sue: 'How to Find Your Fairy Name' and 'St George's Day Rhyme' by permission of the author; D'Arcy, Brian: 'Sea Fairies' and 'Sugar Plum Fairies Dance' by permission of the author; Dixon, Peter: 'Fairy Picnic' first published in *The Tortoise Had a Mighty Roar*, Macmillan Children's Books (2005), by permission of the author; Douthwaite, Gina: 'Winter Window' first published in *Magic*, Scholastic (1998), by permission of the author; Finney, Eric: 'Will o' the Wisp', 'Flower Fairies', 'Pilliwiggin', 'Dryad', 'Bean Tighe', 'Churnmilk Peg', 'Alp Luachra' and 'Leprechaun' all by permission of the author; Houston, Libby: 'Tam Lin' first published in *Tam Lin and Other Tales*, Greville Press (2005), by permission of the author; Leighton, Patricia: 'Who Believes in Fairies?' first published in *Young Hippo Magic Poems*, Scholastic (1997), 'A Gift from the Fairies', 'Dance of Death' and 'A Far Journey' all by permission of the author; Rice, John: 'The Cauldron of Sunset' first published in *The Dream of Night Fishes*, Scottish Cultural Press (1998), 'A Fairy Carol for Summer', 'Instructions for Spotting and Trapping a Fairy', 'Faery Flights' and 'The Kelpie of Loch Coruisk' all by permission of the author; Simpson, Matt: 'Fairy Song' by permission of the author; Swinger, Marian: 'The Fairy Queen', 'A Fairy's Revenge' and 'The Girl Who Could See Fairies' all by permission of the author; Townsend, Jill: 'Tooth Fairy' by permission of the author; Warren, Celia: 'Fairies in the Garden' copyright © Celia Warren 2006 by permission of the author; Webster, Clive: 'The Fairy and the Foxglove' by permission of the author.

Every effort has been made to trace the copyright holders but if any have been inadvertently overlooked the publishers will be pleased to make the necessary arrangement at the first opportunity.